The Parents of Flannery McKracken copyright © 2009 by Accord Publishing,
a division of Andrews McMeel Publishing, LLC. All rights reserved. Printed in Korea.
No part of this book may be used or reproduced in any manner
whatsoever without written permission except in the case of reprints
in the context of reviews. For information, write
Accord Publishing, 1404 Larimer Street, Suite 200, Denver, CO 80202.

09 10 11 12 13 14 PCK 09 08 07 06 05 04 03 02 01

www.accordpublishing.com

ISBN-13: 978-0-7407-8429-3
ISBN-10: 0-7407-8429-3

Library of Congress Control Number: 2009921305

The Parents of Flannery McKracken

by
Gary Wise

 **A**CCORD **PUBLISHING**
a division of Andrews McMeel Publishing, LLC
Denver, Colorado

The Parents of Flannery McKracken ...

… wake cheerfully each morning. Time to get a move on!
Lift that barge! Tote that bale! Brush those teeth!
So say the parents of Flannery McKracken.

Flannery McKracken does not wake early (excluding weekends, holidays, vacation days, and other non-school days).

It is at this point you should know something about Flannery McKracken early in the morning. She is slooooooooooooooooooooooooooooooooooooooo oooooooooooooooooooooooooooooooooooooooooo oooooooooooooooooooooooooooooooooooooooooo ooooooooooooooooooooooowwwwwwwwwwww.

To get her out of bed, the parents of Flannery McKracken use a cannon.

To get Flannery McKracken into the bathroom requires a rhinoceros for pushing and an elephant for pulling.

To brush her teeth, the parents of
Flannery McKracken have installed
an automatic, computerized,
stainless steel jiggling stool.

To get her dressed, oh my …
to get Flannery McKracken dressed,
now that takes some doing.

To make her stand up straight, the parents of
Flannery McKracken keep a marching band.
They play the national anthem.

To actually, physically, get real clothes on
Flannery McKracken takes seven Fairy Godmothers
with magic wands and the patience of saints.

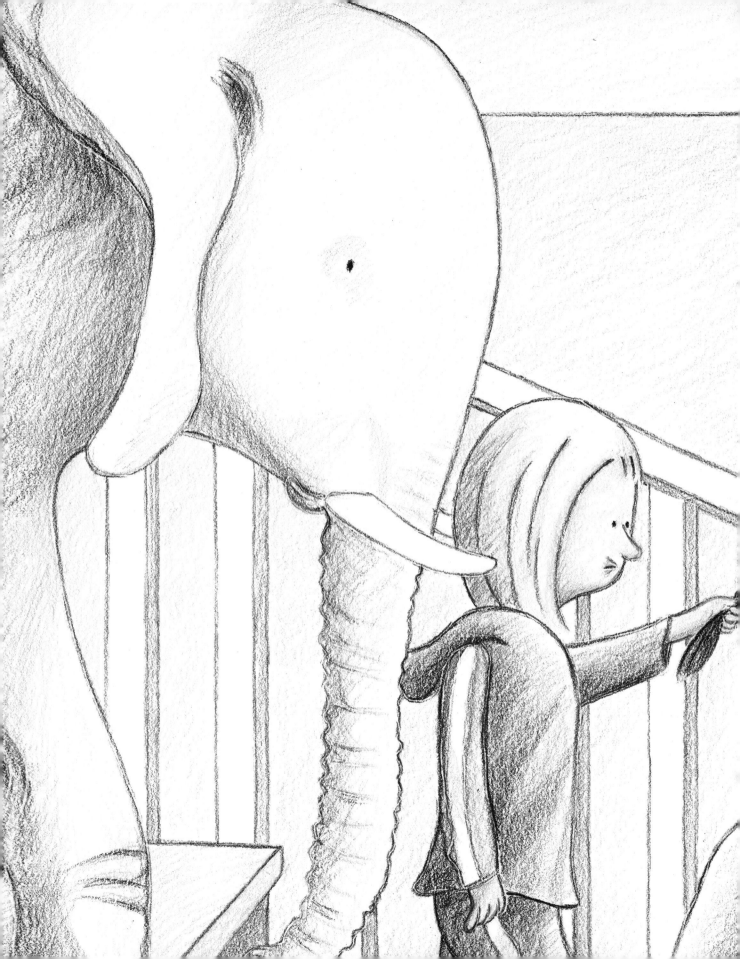

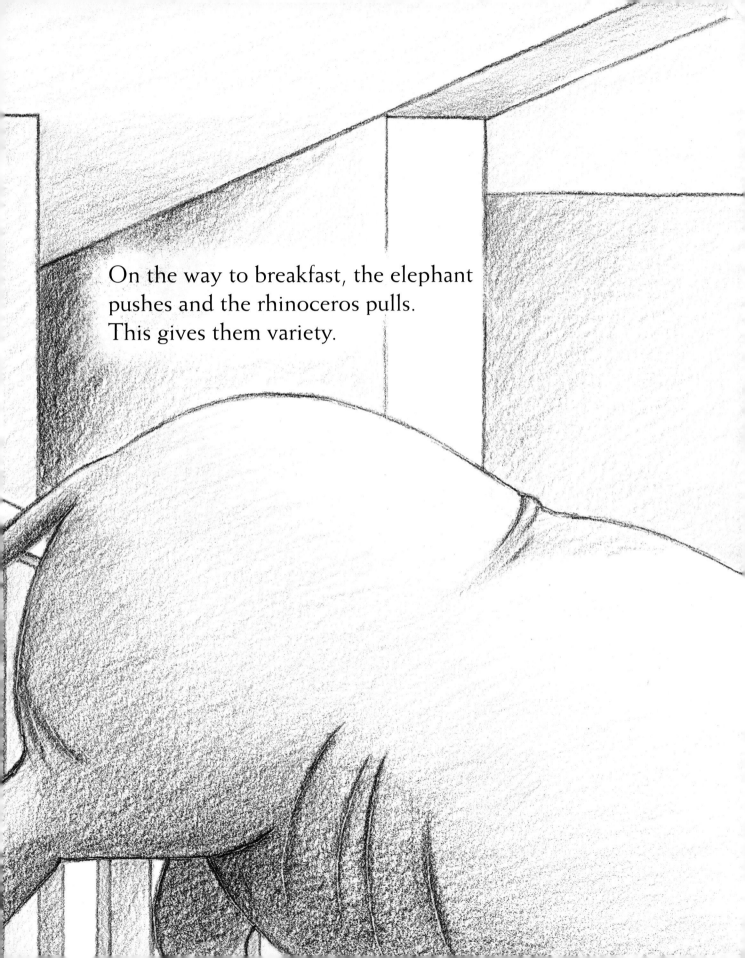

On the way to breakfast, the elephant
pushes and the rhinoceros pulls.
This gives them variety.

A family of monkeys is employed by the parents of Flannery McKracken. They keep the spoon alternating between cereal bowl and mouth. Juice is administered through a tube.

De-splattering, de-crumbing, de-milk-mustaching and hair-doing are handled by the "ChildVac Pro Grooming Model II," recently leased by the parents of Flannery McKracken.

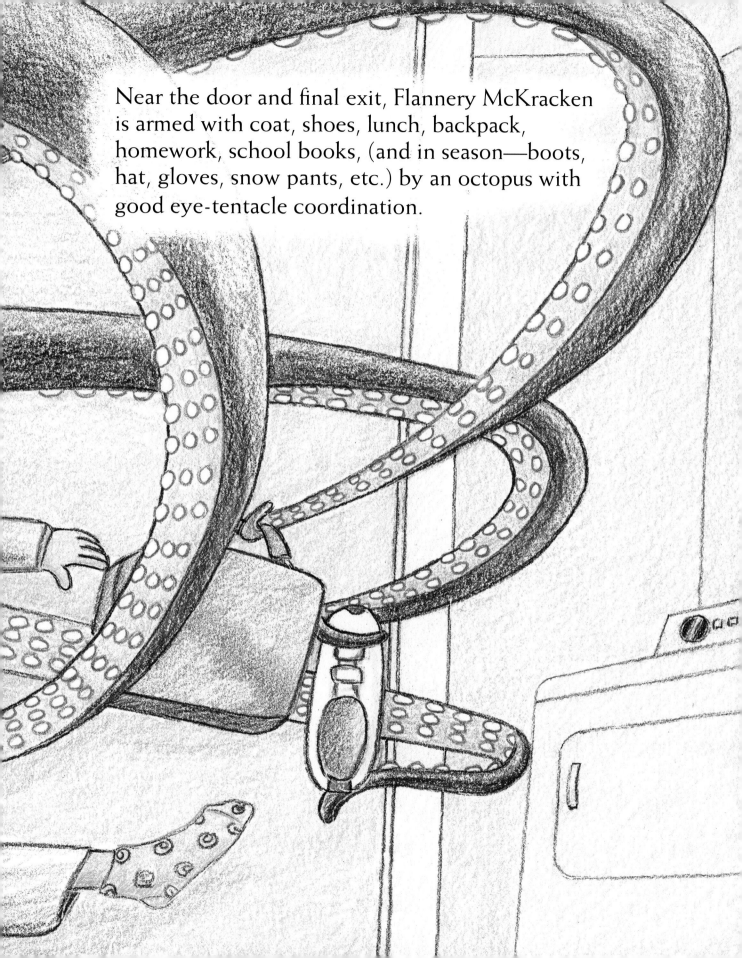

Near the door and final exit, Flannery McKracken is armed with coat, shoes, lunch, backpack, homework, school books, (and in season—boots, hat, gloves, snow pants, etc.) by an octopus with good eye-tentacle coordination.

The parents of Flannery McKracken supply
the final touch, a kiss on each cheek.

How they get her moving at school is anybody's guess.